A
**BUTCH
BLISS**
NOVELLA

Also by Harry Bryant

Hidden Palms
Snake Road
The Right Kind of Sinner

IN

&

OUT

HARRY BRYANT

51325 Books

This book was printed in the United States of America. It is a product of Firebird Creative (Clackamas, OR).

What are you going to do first?

Book Design by Mark Teppo
Copy Edit by Shannon Page

First **51325 Books** edition: January 2018.

IN
&
OUT

CHAPTER 1

EVENTUALLY, I WAS ALLOWED TO LEAVE CDCR'S PUBLICLY -funded school for wayward boys.

"One watch, Swatch. Red. One wallet, leather." The uniform in the cage wasn't going to be hurried. This was his gig, and doling out a prisoner's—ex-prisoner, now—personal effects was yet another opportunity for the California Department of Corrections and Rehabilitation to remind cons who was in charge. "One California driver's license: expired. One credit card: expired. One grocery store club card: no expiration date."

This guy—his name tag read "Doyle"—hadn't been here when I had checked in a decade ago, and the previous master of the plastic inventory bags had been particular and exacting in his accounting. A wallet wasn't just a wallet; it was a piece of leather with lots and lots of stuff inside.

"One business card for a law firm in West Hollywood."

Trent, Baylor, & Howe. Baylor had been my lawyer. He had been apologetic about losing the case which had landed me in jail, and had remained in touch for a while. Always promising that he was working on a retrial. *Gonna happen any day, Bliss, I promise.* Of course, after the incident in the shower, the topic never came up in my conversations with him. Even though he got the charge reduced to Involuntary Manslaughter, it was still another five years added to my sentence.

After that, I didn't hear much from Baylor. He had to chase paying clients. I didn't blame him.

"One condom." Doyle paused and glanced up at me. His beady eyes twinkled as he smirked. "Probably expired."

"Only one way to find out," I offered.

The fleshy folds around his eyes tightened and the smirk slid off his face. He dropped the silver-wrapped condom in the metal tray on his side of the cage, dusting off his fingers like he had touched something vile.

"One ATM card: no expiration date. One auto insurance card: expired," he said, continuing his inventory. "One picture: brunette." He peered at me, his eyes hooded now. "Relationship status: expired."

"That might be a picture of my sister," I pointed out. "I'm sure she still likes me."

The guard standing next to me shifted his weight from side to side. His name was Halter; we called him "Halt or!" Most of the first block had tasted his Taser. He liked shouting that catch phrase just before he zapped a recalcitrant inmate. I had to give him some credit, though. We did stop what we were doing—standing around, playing ball, beating the shit out of each other—when Halter told us to. Shock treatment behavior modification works, even if the state doesn't bother putting that in its annual reports. No reason to get the frosted-tip, recently-manicured, well-intentioned society set all in a tither.

They like their Vasoline-lensed version of prison life more than the less-than-savory reality of what actually goes on inside state correctional facilities.

Halter cleared his throat and made a production out of looking at his watch, which was not as cheap and out of date as mine. But then again, he got to leave Tehachapi every night. He got to walk through the iron-barred gate on the far side of this room; stroll out to his car, which he a) could legally drive, and b) had insurance for; and go home to a wife or girlfriend, who was probably more eager to go on and on about what she had bought at the mall than to hear Halter talk about how inmates pissed themselves when they got lit up with several thousand volts of electrical current.

Unlike Halter, I wasn't in any rush. I had been patient for three thousand, six hundred, and seventy days so far. I could wait out Doyle's lugubrious reading of the inventory sheet.

Waiting was the only thing that wouldn't kill you in prison. Everything else? Well, you do what you have to do to survive inside, and when you get out, you leave it behind. If you're smart, you just walk away from the concrete walls, artificial lighting, stale farts, and the lingering malaise of poisonous captivity.

I was going to try to be smart.

"Two hundred and six dollars, in various denominations," Doyle said. He counted the money twice before putting it in the tray.

Halter glanced at me, an eyebrow raised.

I didn't bother to mention there had been more than five hundred in my wallet when I had left my apartment that night. And yes, I had stopped on Sunset for burgers and shakes—it was important to show up at Creed's place with food, after all—but that was mere pocket change, right?

"Eighty-six cents, in various coins." Doyle dribbled the coins into the tray.

"What's a cup of coffee cost these days?" I asked Halter.

"More than a buck. Less than two hundred."

"Well, I should be good for one day, at least," I said. "Maybe two."

"You'll be back within the week," he said.

"I can't imagine why," I said. "Oh, unless it's for fucking your girlfriend. No, wait. Is it legal if she's sixteen? I can't remember."

His eyes narrowed, and his hand dropped to the Taser holstered on his belt. I looked at his hand and then directed my attention to Doyle's fat face. "You remember what happened the last time you pulled that on me?" I asked Halter. "I'm a lot closer to you this time."

Doyle shoved the metal tray through the slot in the cage. "Sign for it," he snapped.

I stepped away from Halter, putting my back to him, and quickly tilted my personal effects into the plastic bag CDCR so politely provided. I folded the bag around my stuff and crammed it into the front pocket of my jeans.

They had already given me back the clothes I had been wearing the night I had arrived. The jeans were baggy in the waist and tight in the thigh. My T-shirt strained across my chest. It had a cartoon character on it, redrawn in a more rebellious pose—beer can in one hand, fat spliff in the other. He was waggling his cartoon tongue, letting the ladies know he could unspool it down past his chin if they asked nicely.

One of the finer reminders on the part of CDCR: *Hey, asshole, you remember when you were dragged here in chains? All blubbery and bummed that you were going to miss a whole bunch of shit for a while? Yeah, guess what? When you get out, you get to walk out wearing whatever stupid-ass attire you had on when you got popped.*

No one ever gets popped when they're wearing their best "I'm just going to the store" track suit.

I signed the release form, acknowledging that I agreed with the State of California's ability to do math on my behalf, and disabusing them of any responsibility for funds that may or may not have gone missing from my personal inventory.

You have time to think about what's really important when your life is nothing more than a cell—nine foot by six foot, complete with a steel toilet that didn't have a lid—and you realize: *Hey, I haven't missed that money in a few years; I probably won't miss it at all.*

C'est la vie, as Mr. Chow used to say. Or, because he's Chinese: *such is fate.*

He had another five to go on his sentence. Income tax evasion, which is the federal government's way of saying: *Ah, fuck it; we can't pin anything with a life sentence on you, so we'll bullshit up some unreported income nonsense just to own a nice chunk of your retirement.*

Such is fate, you know?

Halter followed me through the iron gate, and we walked down a white hall. There were windows along the left-hand side, up near the ceiling, which let glorious California sunshine stream in. The windows were up high enough you couldn't see out of them. No reason to give you a view. You were going to be outside soon enough, where you could dawdle and gawk on your own damn time.

Your own damn time. Such a strange notion.

What are you going to do first? Tattoo Bob had wanted to know during my last day in the yard. Once I got within seventy-two hours of being released, it was standard procedure to keep me out of gen pop, and so this session with the weights was the closest thing I'd get to a goodbye party.

When you get out, Bob asked. *What are you going to do?*

Me'n'Sally are gonna— Dicky started.

We all know what you're going to do, Bob said. *Shit, the whole world knows what you're going to do. Except Sally. She doesn't know.*

Fuck you, Bob. She's waiting for me. She's gonna be there.

I'm going to have a beer, Lin offered, interrupting an argument that had been going on for over a year. *Tecate. With lime. No, fuck that. I'm going to have six. And then I'm going to puke.*

Dicky had found that extremely funny. Or maybe he was thinking about how he was going to stick his thumb in Bob's eye. It was hard to tell with Dicky sometimes.

Mr. Chow kept doing *tai chi*. Stoic as a bat.

I'm going to In-N-Out Burger, Bob said. He tapped the right-angled arrow tattoo on the inside of his right bicep.

Bob had many tattoos, most of which had been hand-applied during his time at Tehachapi, and most of which were logos of the things he missed. Bob wasn't about to let the Man take away his consumer identity.

I'm going to walk, I said. *And I'm going to keep walking until there is no more road.*

Why? Dicky asked, his face all screwed up as he tried to figure out what the hell I was talking about.

Because he can, Mr. Chow said.

He smiled at me, and I felt like a ten-year-old boy who had just been told by his father that maybe he wasn't going to disappoint him after all.

The door at the end of the white hall was a couple of inches thick, and there was a small reinforced glass port set in it. I stopped about ten feet from the door, and looked up at the surveillance camera mounted in the corner. I heard Halter stop behind me, and I tried really hard not to let my shoulders twitch. I was almost out. Don't give him any final satisfaction.

A buzzer sounded in the wall, and bolts clacked back. The door swung open, and Halter couldn't help but tap me on the shoulder one last time. I twitched, and let it go. I was still on this side of the door. I wasn't free yet.

Past the door was a tiny waiting room, sectioned off from a larger room by another set of iron bars. Halter stopped on the threshold behind me. "See you next week, asshole," he said.

"I'll send you a card at Christmas," I said, moving out of the way of the heavy door as it pivoted back into place. The bolts shot home again, and the buzzer sounded once more. Halter watched me through the tiny window, and I gave him a friendly wave before I turned away. Showing him my back. Leaving behind the white hall, the ugly concrete block, my cell, and Dicky and Bob and Lin and Mr. Chow.

A couple of guards waited on the other side of the cage, and one of them put a key in the heavy lock. He pulled the gate open, and motioned that I should walk out. One of the other guards had a clipboard in his hand, and he checked it against a visual examination of my face. "Robert Bliss," he said, and then he rattled off a string of numbers that was my CDCR-provided identification.

"That's me," I said.

He held out the clipboard and a pen. "Sign at the bottom."

I signed.

"Keep the pen," he said. "Think of it as a souvenir."

I looked at the third guy, who was standing over by a beige door with a funny-looking bar across it. A crash-bar, they were called. To make it easy to push the door open in an emergency. I almost laughed at the sight of it. Doors weren't supposed to be easy to open.

"We done here?" I asked him.

"You're done," he said. He pushed his way through the door and held it open for me. I stared at the bright sunlight streaming into the waiting room. I was almost afraid to walk into it. Like I might burst into flames or something.

I looked at the guy with the clipboard. "I'm done," I said, and I dropped the pen on the floor. "Oops."

Clipboard guy glared at me, but he didn't say anything or do anything.

I waited a beat or six, savoring the thrill racing through my blood. And then, before I did something stupid, I walked into the light, and out of prison.

CHAPTER 2

I STOOD AT THE EDGE OF THE PARKING LOT. BEHIND ME were the unmarked concrete buildings of the Tehachapi Correctional Facility. There were signs warning tourists and other folks who might be wondering what was going on behind the twelve-foot-high chain link fence, all topped about with razor wire. This area was under the authoritarian gaze of the California Department of Corrections and Rehabilitation. Nothing to see. Move the fuck on.

Distantly, I heard a buzz, followed by the muffled sound of an amplified voice. Rotation time in the yard. They didn't want us to burn in what sun we got inside the concrete-walled yard.

I counted cars in the parking lot, which was bigger than the yard. In fact, if I were to walk across the parking lot, I would walk farther in a straight line than I had been able to do in ten years. I shuffled my feet, dragging them along the white line painted at the edge of the lot. Should I? I could. No one would stop me.

I stepped across the white line, and my shoulders tensed. I was waiting to hear the sound of a guard's voice, or maybe even the farting noise of Halter's Taser as it fired its little darts.

Nothing happened. The sun continued to beat down on me. A mercurial breeze rolled a cloud of dust across the lot. A pair of flickers darted across the sky.

I shook out my shoulders and took another step. And then another. Still nothing. I kept walking, my pace increasing until I was running. My arms pumping. My breath fast and loose in my throat. The other side of the parking lot was right over there. I could make it. I could run as fast and as far as I wanted. I didn't have to stop on the white line. I could keep going. Just like I told the gang in the yard. *I'm going to keep walking until there is no more road.*

Fuck walking. I was going to run.

Except that stitch in my side was really hurting, and I was getting light-headed.

I stopped shy of the white line that was the far boundary of the parking lot, and walked the last few yards. There was sweat on my face and chest, and my lungs were working hard. It wasn't even a hundred-yard dash, but it was a dash nonetheless. If I had a list of post-prison to-dos, I could cross *Run Like You Just Don't Care* off the list.

As I stood next to the line, catching my breath, a black car turned into the parking lot. Its muffler wasn't up to the job, and the engine rattled and grumbled as the car drove down the lane closest to the prison and pulled into an empty spot. The car backfired once before the driver switched off the engine, and a short guy with a disheveled mass of curly brown hair popped out of the vehicle.

He wore black sunglasses with enormous lenses that made him look like a bug, and a striped tank top and cut-off jean shorts. He walked around the front of his car, then stopped when he didn't see anyone standing near the prison gate. He turned, caught sight of me, and waved frantically.

Before I could say or do anything, he darted back to his car, started it up, and pulled out of the parking spot. He drove to the end of the lane, and then came down to me. The wheels crunched across loose gravel as the car slowly rolled to a stop. It was a late-seventies Trans Am, not unlike the one I had driven out to California from Colorado, back when I had come west to find fame and fortune in Hollywood. This one had been painted black in an effort to hide some not entirely professional body work.

The driver's-side window rolled down, and the curly-haired guy with the bug glasses gave me a gap-toothed smile. Only then did I recognize him.

"Hey, Tex," I said.

"Bliss!" he crowed. "You're out!"

"I am."

"Looks like I got here just in time. You been waiting long?"

"No," I said. "Just a few minutes."

"Cool. Cool." He nodded, like he was listening to music only he could hear. "Get in, man. We got some driving to do."

I looked around the lot. "There's supposed to be a bus," I said. "Runs from Bakersfield to Mojave. It should be along pretty soon."

"Oh, man. Fuck the bus. I'm your ride."

I tongued the inside of my cheek as I gave Tex a good eyeballing. His real name was Dexter, but his screen name was Tex. Tex Western. His big break had been on a Western knockoff. *Cowpoke*. With all the requisite jokes about having sex with farm animals, of course. This wasn't high art, after all, and if you had to think about the punchline, then the jokes weren't working. *If I'm not laughing, I should be thinking about sex*, one director had been fond of shouting at the actors. *If I'm having sex, I shouldn't be laughing. It's a simple as that.*

Cowpoke did well for Tex. So did *Cowpoke 2: The Wrangling* and *Cowpoke 3: Mastering the Herd*. They were probably up to *Cowpoke 10* or *12* by now. When a formula worked, why change anything?

"It's been a long time, Tex," I said. "No calls. No cards. And yet, here you are. Picking me up like I'm your prom date or something."

"Aw, don't be like that, Bliss. I kept tabs on you. I called last week, and they told me when you were being released. Why wouldn't I be here?"

"You weren't there last time."

He hung his head, his fingers dancing on the steering wheel. "Man. Don't think a day goes by that I don't thank God about that. But come on, Bliss. It was Dahlia." His shoulders jerked as he laughed. "Shit, that was my one chance. After that night . . ."

He looked up at me. "Come on, Bliss. Get in the car. It's three hours back to LA. It'll take all fucking day and night if you wait for the bus."

"Maybe I'm not going back to LA," I said.

He laughed. "No? Where else are you going to go?"

He had a point.

Ten years ago, Tex and I had been young and dumb and full of—well, you know the saying. And it was doubly true for fresh studs in the *adult filmed entertainment industry*, as we were supposed to call it. Porn was finally hitting the mainstream. Films were getting shown in theaters; actors could admit to their neighbors and friends that they fucked other actors for a living. Some of us were starting to be recognized on the street by fans. There was a lot of money going around, and a lot of pressure to perform. As long as you could rise to the occasion, there was work. If you couldn't, well, someone younger could take your place. A decent set of abs helped, as did a nice chiseled jaw. No one gave a shit if you could remember your lines or say them convincingly. As long as you dropped your pants and saluted on command, you could stay in the frame. Or, at least, part of you could.

If we weren't shooting, we were partying, and a bunch of us had ended up at a house up in Laurel Canyon. Some producer's mansion. A dozen rooms. Big pool. The studio had probably shot a film or two there. Hell, you could shoot a couple of films simultaneously and none of the crews would get in each other's way. That sort of place.

Anyway, we had run out of drugs—which happens more often than you'd think with these impromptu parties. *Hey, let's all meet at this address and drink and snort and smoke and do whatever else we can find.* Cue the collective cheer and the long line of cars gliding up into the posh canyon.

Because I knew a guy, I had been tapped to go fetch more drugs. I had taken a collection, and scared up a little over five hundred dollars. Not much, and certainly not enough to keep the party going all night, but like I said, I knew the guy. There was some hope that I could negotiate a better price or get some stuff on credit or some other fucking idiotic idea that was spawned by the collective brain drain floating in the pool that night.

My car had been blocked in by someone's sporty little Mazda. I traded keys and went tearing down the hill in this RX-7, which was a two-door coupe that sounded like it had a swarm of bees under the hood.

Tex didn't go with me, even though there's a rule that you never go alone. You always take a co-pilot. Someone to help you read the traffic signs. Keep you from getting too distracted or too paranoid. Someone who could totally vouch for you if shit got ugly.

And I didn't blame him for bailing on me. Dahlia was a beautiful woman, and many of us had worked with her on-screen. Tex was one of the few who hadn't, and there was a mighty attraction there. Something you can't have very quickly becomes something you have to have. And so after swapping keys with the studio guy who owned the Mazda, I had passed through the kitchen. Dahlia was sitting on the counter, her long legs wrapped around Tex. *You coming?* I had asked.

Give me a few minutes, he said, and she giggled in that heart-stopping way of hers.

I didn't feel like waiting.

Creed's place was in West Hollywood. I had stopped at an In-N-Out Burger on Sunset and called ahead. *And bring some burgers*, Creed had said. And he hadn't laughed at me when I had suggested I wouldn't mind a little advance.

Creed was in a mood. At the time, I was too keyed up and stoned to notice, and it was only a few months later, after I was good and settled in my cell at Tehachapi, that I figured out why he had been on edge. *Sure*, he said, when I asked about getting some coke on account. *Do me a favor, and I'll give you some stuff. Gratis.*

He just needed me to run some bags over to Central. *Nothing complicated. Two bags. Here's the address. Guy will answer the door. He'll ask you about your mother. You tell him she moved to Tulsa and married a vacuum salesman. He'll say, 'That sucks,' and you'll both laugh. Got it?*

I got it, along with a couple grams of coke and a big bag of weed. We didn't even talk about the five hundred dollars in my wallet.

Two miles from his house, some jackass ran a red light and clipped the back end of the Mazda. Stupid little car spun like a top across the intersection and hopped the curb. Banged over a fire hydrant and tried to head-butt an old oak. I got bounced around inside the car, and by the time I rewound the last thirty seconds and figured out what happened, the intersection had filled up with cops. They had lots of questions about the two duffels in the trunk and the bag of weed that exploded all over the interior of the car.

Did I blame Tex for not riding along? If he had, he'd have been bent over the hood of a car, cuffed, hearing his rights read like hearing a bored waitress reeling off the happy hour specials, and spending the next ten years in jail too. There was never any point in being angry at him; oh, but that didn't stop me. I had lots of time to be angry at a lot of people, and I gave them all equal accounting. None of it changed my course, though, and none of it made the hours and days and weeks go by any faster.

C'est la vie.

CHAPTER 3

TEX WAS OF THE OPINION THAT WHAT I WANTED MORE than anything was to hear all the news from the last decade, and he started talking as soon as we pulled out of the parking lot at Tehachapi. I tried once or twice to interrupt him, and finally gave up. Instead, I watched the austere landscape of the Mojave Desert roll by, nodding and grunting occasionally to keep him from repeating himself.

For the first hour, he ran me through a handful of ladies who had, in series, cheated on him with his landlord, stolen a couple thousand in cash while they were in Vegas and left him with the hotel bill, and broken his heart. The last one had almost made him a better man, and he still thought about getting out of the business and going off in search of her, but there was always some excuse that kept him from doing so. Her name was Raquel—like the movie star—and she had been in pharmacy sales or something. The company got bought by some ginormous global brand, and she had moved back east to take over a territory that covered upper New England. *Fucking winters were brutal*, Tex said, *snow up to your waist. People fell down and died while trying to get their mail. Bodies wouldn't be found until mid-spring when the snows finally melted.*

It snowed in the Sierra Nevadas, and every once in a while, there would be a light dusting in the yard, but I hadn't seen real snow in a long time—drifts burying cars, ice bowing trees over, skies so white you thought the world had ended.

As we passed through Mojave, Tex came around to talk about the old business: who was still running a studio; who was fucking who—on and off camera; what kinks had come and gone.

And the production company that owned Cowpoke—Dongle Studios—oh, those guys were bastards, all right. They had cheated him out of a bunch of profit-sharing for the Cowpoke movies, and then, when he had thrown a disc out in his back, had dumped him. And he had injured himself while shooting for a film for them, the fucks! And it wasn't his fault the doctor insisted on six weeks of bed rest. You think he liked lying on his back all day?

Do you know how many films you can shoot in six weeks? he had asked as Mojave receded in the rearview mirror.

I didn't know, and by the time we hit the outskirts of Lancaster, I definitely knew more than I cared to know about the burgeoning direct-to-video market. Film was expensive, and all claims to high art aside, distribution was a pain in the ass, and unless you were filling most of the seats at each showing, you weren't worth the theater's time. The direct market with videotape? That was another thing entirely.

Palmdale: "There's another studio every week. Cameras are getting cheaper all the time, especially if you're shooting video. And the shit you can do on computers these days? Get a couple of cameras and offer some tech wonk free blowjobs for a month, and boom! There's your content pipe. People dig watching porn in their own houses. You can jack off by yourself. Invite a few friends over. Whatever. No one needs to know. Studios are cranking out films as fast as they can, and it ain't fast enough."

San Fernando: "I miss a real plot, you know? With this direct-to-video stuff, it's all about maximizing the T&A— tits and ass, right?—in a ninety-minute film. When you're cramming a half-dozen scenes in, you don't have time for character development. I shot a film last week where there wasn't a script. Nothing. Just some notes about mood and tone. Can you believe that crap? Mood in a porno. Here's a question for you: is there fucking, yes or no? That's all the mood you need."

Sherman Oaks, after switching over to the 405 and hitting rush hour traffic: "There were some dark times there, after you went to jail. The dickhead DA wanted to shut the industry down, man. You were a poster child for sinning, Bliss. Drugs. Dicks. Pussy. All three at the same time. Who knows what sort of crazy shit we were trying to seduce America's kids with. All across LA County, man. Orange, too. It was a wasteland of degradation and wanton sinning, and that guy? He was going to show us, wasn't he? He was going to clean it all up. Starting with you—poor fucking poster boy. He was going to save you, even if it meant sending you to jail where—come on, let's get serious; you weren't going to get less action in jail, were you? I mean, not that you were into the queer stuff, anyway. But, you know—and your lawyer? What the fuck did he do for you? That case was utter bullshit, and he plea bargained you to what? Five years? Man, I hope you didn't pay your lawyer, because man, he fucked you too. I mean, not really, but, you know, metaphorically. Or whatever."

And when he got off on Sepulveda and turned up Mountaingate Drive, I asked my first question: "Where are we going?"

The valley had changed in the last decade. It used to be the end of the world, but there was more concrete and steel running along the highway than I remembered, and it had all been . . . gentrified. Gone were the cheap strip malls of tattoo parlors, nail salons, and bail bondsmen. Now there were franchise restaurants, parking lots, and indoor malls. Mountaingate hadn't changed all that much: the houses were still twice as large as anything closer to the freeway, and the gates were still iron and brick.

"There's a party going on up here," Tex said.

"There's always a party."

"Yeah, I know. But I want you to meet some people."

"And they're going to be at this party?"

He grinned, showing nice crisp dental caps, along with that gap in the front. Focus group testing had revealed that women liked the slightly less than perfect physique. Well, above the waist, that is.

"It's where business gets done, man," he said.

"So it's *that* sort of meeting."

He slowed down, peering at the numbers of the houses. "Just be chill, Bliss. Everything is going to be great."

I pointed at the cars parked two and three deep along the road. "It's up there."

"Right, right." He laughed as he eased his car over to the shoulder of the road. "Look at you, eagle eye."

He talked a lot when he was nervous, and I had been wondering for a while what was making him squirm. Now I had an inkling, and when he switched off the car, I made no move to get out. Tex ran his hands through his hair and gave me a bug-eyed look. "You ready?"

"What is this, Tex?"

"It's a party."

I shook my head. "I've been out of prison less than five hours, and you're hauling me to a meet and greet. What's the rush?"

"You're out, man. I thought we should celebrate, you know? Freedom and all that bullshit. Get you some pussy. Have a drink or two or a dozen. I don't care. You're not driving, right?" He laughed, and there was too much tension riding in the back of his throat.

I didn't like that I couldn't see his eyes. You can tell a lot about what a man's thinking by watching his eyes. Tex's bug glasses hid too much of his face.

Shaking my head, I got out of the car and closed the door. There were a lot of expensive cars crammed along the street, and I could hear voices laughing and shouting, along with the *thump thump thump* of a massive stereo system. "It's a big party," I said.

Tex spread his hands and let them rest on the top of his car. "He's kind of a big deal."

"Who?"

"The guy who owns this house."

"Anyone I know?"

"You remember Prengle? Austin Prengle? Directed a couple of films before getting into the production and distribution side of things. Silver Tuna. You remember it?"

I shook my head.

Tex nodded toward the music and laughter. "He bought a manufacturing plant, where he could churn out videotapes by the thousands. Convinced a couple other guys like him—less than a dozen films each, you know?—talked them into letting him do replication and distribution, for a percentage. Five points here. Ten points there. It adds up. A couple years later, he owns the distribution channel. You want to get your films in every mom and pop video store across America? You deal with Silver Tuna, and you take whatever distribution Prengle feels like offering you."

"Are you making your own studio? Going to get behind the camera?"

"No, man. That's a lot of paperwork and bullshit I don't need. I'm just here for the opportunities." He smiled at me. "And the pussy."

I eyed him. "You must not be working, if that's the line you're selling."

"I'm getting more than you," he said. "And I did some work last week. Remember? *Mood Poem #9* or some shit. I don't even remember what it was called."

"Everyone has been getting more than me," I said.

He drummed his hands on the roof of his car. "Maybe this is your lucky night, then."

"This wasn't the first thing I wanted to do after I got out of prison."

"No? It should be."

"It's not even in the top five, frankly."

He made a face. "You switch teams or something? You drop the soap too many times in the shower?"

"You don't get soap. Not like that. It comes out of a dispenser, mounted on the wall."

"Whatever. You know what I mean."

"No, Tex, I haven't switched teams."

"That's good, 'cause there is bound to be some mighty fine p—"

"Tex. Give it a rest."

He held up his hands. "Okay, okay. I hear you. Let's just go up and have a good time, all right?"

I looked up the hill, and then at him, and then back the way we had come. It was a mile or two back to the base of the road. There wasn't much in the way of services at the 405 interchange, but I could find a phone somewhere. Call a cab. Have them take me . . .

Take me where, really? Among the papers that Baylor had me sign after I got sent up to Tehachapi had been a bunch of documents that had taken care of my apartment and my stuff. Lease ran out. Stuff went into storage. What stuff that was worth storing, that is, and right now, I couldn't think of anything that had been worth keeping in a box somewhere. I was, technically, homeless. Of course, Trent, Baylor, & Howe would take my call, and they'd probably help me find a place to live and all that, but it was after business hours. They hadn't been the types to work late back then, and I doubted they were now. Even if I called the firm tonight, they wouldn't get back to me until tomorrow morning. Until then, I was either on my own or . . . hanging out with Tex. At some party, up on the hill overlooking the 405.

I still hadn't seen LA proper yet.

"Yeah, all right," I said. "Let's go have a good time."

"Rock and roll," he chortled. "That's more like it." He whooped and did a little shimmy as he danced toward the music.

A pair of guys in matching shirts and haircuts stood next to a valet station at the front gate, and Tex waved them off when they offered to take his keys. The driveway wound through a heavily sculpted lawn—lots of grass, rock formations, and more distinct tree species than were indigenous to southern California. The music got louder as we went farther back from the road; I could hear the occasional snippet of a female voice, along with lots of processed electronics. It was a remix of some kind, reworking some hit from the past decade into a rhythmic loop that sounded like it could go on all night.

We caught glimpses of the house—or parts of the house, really. It was wider than it was tall, and it was modeled after a European carriage house. There were three sets of garage doors, and each looked like they could fit two cars. A wide series of steps led up to a tall entry, and the door was wide open, letting out all the light and sound. Many of the windows were bright with light too.

Past the far wing was a separate house—a modest two-story affair—and past that was a tennis court and a grassy field. I paused at the base of the porch steps, peering toward the group of small people clustered on the field. "Is that a pony?"

Tex looked too. "Yeah, man, pony rides!"

"You can't put adults on ponies," I said. "We weigh too much."

"Dwarves! He's got dwarves."

I looked at him. "It's kids," I said. "The pony rides are for kids."

He wrinkled his nose. "You don't bring kids to a party like this. It's got to be dwarves." He waved a hand toward the field. "Go look, man. But I'm telling you. It's little people."

I eyed the open door of the house. There was quite the party going on, and I wasn't sure I was ready to deal with all of that. The light. The noise. The people. A shiver ran down my spine, and I took an involuntary step back. "Yeah, maybe I'll start over there," I said. "Little people might be all I can handle right now."

"Right on. Come find me later, okay? I'll be at the bar. The one by the pool."

I nodded, filing that detail away. Naturally, a party like this would have more than one bar. *Welcome back to civilization, Bliss*, I thought as I walked along a path of wide paving stones that looped along the front of the main house. *Hell of a mother-in-law condo*, I thought as I wandered past the smaller building.

A mixed group of men and women were pretending to play triples at tennis, though it was mostly the four dudes trying to hit each other with balls while the two women stood at the net and made out. I stopped and watched them curl their tongues. It had been a while since I had seen such a remarkable sight, and it didn't take long for my appreciation of their efforts to become embarrassingly evident, and I stumped past the court.

There was a pony in the field, and the small people queuing up for rides were, in fact, kids and not dwarves. Six of them, and they were all not very good at waiting.

The woman leading the pony was lanky and lean. Her hair was long and blond—a little lighter than the pony's mane—and it fell down her back in a loose braid. She wore jeans, a leather vest, and a blue and red checked shirt. She looked at me as she brought the pony around to the cluster of kids, and there was both keen interest and a pent-up restlessness in her green eyes.

"Hi," I said.

It'd been a long time since I'd talked with a girl. I figured I should start out easy.

She helped the rosy-cheeked kid off the pony, and passed over the obnoxious kid who had shoved her way to the front of the queue and pointed at the sad-faced kid in the back. The kid's face brightened, and the woman helped her up onto the saddle. The pony looked at me through a fringe of long hair as it ambled along the track its hooves had worn in the grass. The woman walked with the pony, her hand resting on the saddle horn.

"Hi," she said as they passed by.

She walked with a hiccup in her step, as if her right leg couldn't bend quite as readily at the hip as her left.

I watched her walk the kid and the pony in a circle, and when they passed the second time, I made more conversation. "I'm Robert," I said.

"Geo," she replied. She nodded at the pony. "Buttercup."

"That short for anything?"

She cocked her head at me. "You in a rush?"

"No," I admitted. "I've got some free time on my hands." And I marveled at how casually I had made that sound. *Free time.*

"Maybe I'll tell you later," she said over her shoulder.

"Okay." My breath was quick in my throat as I realized I had something to look forward to.

When was the last time I looked forward to anything? You stayed in the moment while you were inside. You didn't think about the life you had before you got there. You didn't dream about the life you were going to have after you got out. You kept your eyes open. You paid attention to what was around you; and when you were in your cell and there was nothing to look at, you learned how to look at nothing until it was time to eat, shit, or sleep. Anticipation was a distraction, and distractions made time slow down. In some cases, they could get you killed. You didn't get distracted. You didn't let anticipation in.

"You okay, mister?" one of the kids asked.

I swiped a hand at my face, brushing the moisture off my cheek. "Yeah, I'm fine," I said. The kid's face said she didn't believe me. "It's been a while since I talked to a pretty girl," I said. "I'm a little nervous."

The only boy in the group nodded tightly when I said this, as if he knew exactly what I was talking about.

"Boys are like that," the pushy girl said. She had a round face and her hair looked like it had been styled earlier in the day at a very expensive salon. She was wearing a red dress and pink tights. "Celeste says they never figure it out."

"Figure what out?" I asked.

"How to talk to girls."

"And who is Celeste?"

"My step-mom."

"Does she live here?"

"Sometimes," the girl said. "Where do you live?"

"Oh, I'm between places," I said, letting my gaze wander toward Geo and Buttercup. She was watching me, a tiny smile curling the corner of her mouth. "I've been away for a while."

"Are you someone important?" another girl asked.

"Gosh, no. I'm nobody."

Buttercup finished her circuit and stopped to munch on some grass as Geo helped the rider off. This time she picked the obnoxious one, who made a big show of getting into the saddle on her own. Buttercup shook her mane as the girl urged her to walk, and Geo trailed after the pony and rider. "You're someone," she said as she walked past. "I can tell by your eyes."

I stared after her for a moment, and then looked over at the boy in the group. "Make eye contact," I said. "It helps."

He nodded sagely, convinced I had just given him one of the secrets of the universe.

CHAPTER 4

EVERY KID GOT TWO RIDES BEFORE GEO TOLD THEM IT WAS TIME for Buttercup to take a break. They pouted and whined, but took the hint when Geo clapped her hands and shooed them off. As they ambled across the lawn, they were met by a man and a woman dressed in white, who expertly shepherded them into a line that quickly disappeared into the small house.

Geo led the pony over to a bucket of water, and once it was done drinking, she offered it an apple. After looping the halter around a metal pole stuck in the ground, she stuck her hands in the back pockets of her jeans and looked at me.

"You're either a creepy stalker or you have no friends. Which is it?"

"I must not have any friends."

"Are you sure you're not a stalker?"

"I'm very bad at it, if I am."

She laughed. "True, but I feel terrible if I've just made you acknowledge that you have no friends."

"I have one," I admitted. "He brought me here."

"And then he ditched you? What kind of friend is that?"

"He understands that I'm an independent type."

"Are you now?" She wandered toward me. Close enough to signal she was enjoying this conversation. "Are you money or talent?"

"Excuse me?"

"There are two types of people who claim they are 'independent.' People with money and people with talent. Which are you?"

"Talent, I guess."

"You don't have any money?"

"I have some."

She laughed again. "Around here, 'some' means 'none.'"

"Then I definitely fall into the 'talent' column."

"Uh-huh," she said. Her teeth worried her lower lip. "I know who owns this place, and I know the sort of business he's in. It's sweet of him to hire me for his kid's party, but I'm not under any illusions about why I'm here."

I glanced toward the house and the noisy party spilling out of it. "Keep the kids distracted and separate from the rest of the house," I said.

She wrapped her arms around her waist as she looked over at the house too. "I get it. They're people too. They grow up. They have kids. They want to have a normal life. Birthdays. Pony rides. Balloons. All that stuff. Meanwhile . . ."

"You don't approve?"

She put up her hands. "It's not my place to judge. People can do what they like with whom they like."

A familiar figure came around the side of the house. He spotted me and headed toward the field, his bug-eyed head bobbing loosely.

"Where'd all the dwarves go?" Tex asked when he reached the grassy field.

"There weren't any," I said. "Just little kids."

"Huh," he said. He glanced over at Buttercup and then returned his attention to Geo. "Hi," he said. "I'm Tex." He stuck out his hand.

"Geo," she said, leaving her hands in her back pockets.

"Three letters," he said. If he noticed her lack of eagerness to touch him, he didn't let it show. "We got three-letter names. You see that, Bliss?"

"I noticed."

She looked at me. "I thought you said your name was 'Robert.'"

"Bliss is my last name," I said.

"I see."

Tex swung his head from side to side, watching us. "Are you two—" he started.

"We're not," I said.

"We're not what?" Geo wanted to know.

"You been standing here this entire time?" Tex asked.

"More or less," I said.

"Jesus, man. She probably thinks you're a pedophile. Or you're going to snatch her and take her to your secret sex dungeon."

"Do you have a secret sex dungeon?" Geo interjected.

"Is that what they used to call a 'fuck pad'?" I asked.

She snorted with laughter as Tex shook his head. "Man, look. I'm sure she's nice and all, but can we get this business done? You can talk about sex dungeons and fuck pads and whatever else you want after that. For the rest of the night, for all I care. Okay?"

"Ooh, all night?" Geo raised an eyebrow. "Promise?"

I blushed lightly, which made her smile widen.

"I'm sorry. There's a meeting thing or something . . ."

"Yeah," she said. "I know how that all works."

"It's his idea." I jerked my thumb at Tex.

"It's going to change everything," Tex said.

"Everything? Really?" She looked at me for confirmation, and I just shrugged.

"That sounds like an important meeting," she said.

"I'm not a fan of meetings," I said.

"No," she said, cocking her head and staring at me. "No, you're not."

We would have been content to stare at each other for a while, but Tex was dancing like a kid who had to pee. "Come on, Bliss . . ."

"I'm sorry," I said again.

"I'm not," Geo said. "Unless you don't come back . . ."

I hesitated, caught on the verge of saying something, but the words didn't quite feel right. I smiled and nodded, opting to leave it at that.

Tex did a little dance as I turned away from Geo and followed him. He waited until we were out of earshot before giving me a huge grin. "I'd hit that," he said. "I'd totally hit that."

I gave him a look, which he ignored, and then as we reached the walk next to the house: "You're going to hit that, aren't you? Your dick didn't fall off in prison, did it?"

The landscaping got more extreme behind the sprawling mansion. There were rock formations that looked like they had been salvaged from a science fiction film set, and banks of colored lights turned the miniature canyons and Disneyland-style mountain peaks into a rainbow-colored landscape. There was more than one pool and more than one bar, and perched above the larger pool was a white tent with a bunch of speakers and a DJ setup. Beyond the man-made landscaping, the property was heavily wooded.

We ducked into the house through a set of open French doors, and found ourselves in a bedroom larger than the block common room at Tehachapi. The carpet was six inches of white shag. The walls were white. The art was white. The three girls playing with each other on the bed were a contrasting range of brown, browner, and dark, and they giggled and gestured for us to join them as we wandered through.

"Later, ladies," Tex said smoothly, blowing them kisses.

I got a little distracted. It had been a really long time since I had seen that much naked female flesh. Tex gave me a knowing grin as we left the bedroom. "Never underestimate the power of pussy," he said.

We went down a hall that kinked left before opening into another room that was half again as large as the bedroom. This room was done up in shades of brown and red, and there were three large televisions arranged along the far wall. A half-dozen sofas were lined up in uneven rows, and a bunch of men were scattered about the seats, intent on the football games playing on the televisions. Three women in bikini tops were working behind a well-stocked bar off to my left.

I paused as we entered the room. If these guys were working in the adult filmed entertainment industry, then it had changed dramatically in the last decade. There were a couple of stringy-looking guys wearing designer sneakers and ballcaps, who looked like they were whooping it up more to be seen than to be showing true team spirit, and the guy in the grey suit sitting at the bar wasn't drinking. The other four dudes were hard guys. Tattoos. Leather jackets. Gold jewelry. Muscles between their ears.

Everyone—other than the guy at the bar—was there to suck up to the black-haired man sitting on the middle couch. He was wearing a blue track suit with white piping, and lying next to him, her feet tucked into his crotch, was a blond woman wearing a sequin-covered dress that wouldn't hit mid-thigh on a good day. He had one hand draped across her thigh, and his fingers looked like fat sausages.

On the rightmost screen, a player dressed in a red uniform threw a long pass to another guy in the same-colored uniform. The receiver ducked around a defender in blue, danced past a second, and then broke into a long run down the sidelines. Everyone shouted and cheered, as if the player could hear their noise through the television. When the receiver crossed the goal line and the screen cut to a stoic-faced referee with his arms raised, the boys in ballcaps popped up, strutting and slapping high-fives.

I looked at Tex, who nervously rocked back and forth on his heels. I'd have to shout at him to be heard over the noise in the room and so I gave him a cold eye instead, but he wouldn't look at me.

One of the ballcap boys noticed us, and pretty soon, everyone was looking in our direction. Track Suit lifted his hand from his lady friend's thigh, and one of the hard guys seated on the couch near us levered himself upright and came over. He motioned with his head that we should step back out into the hall, and Tex dutifully complied. The hard guy stared at me, and I did my best to not let him get under my skin.

A man can leave prison, but it takes a little while for prison to leave the man.

Out in the hall, the guy leaned against the wall and spread his hands like he was waiting to hear our pitch. "What's on your mind, Tex?" he asked.

"Hey, Largo. I was hoping to get a chance to chat with Mr. Benelli."

"He's watching the game," Largo said.

"Yeah, I see that. I won't be long. Maybe during a commercial break or something . . . ?"

"Whatcha need, Tex?"

Tex pouted for a second, and then realizing that wasn't going to get him anywhere with the big man, he switched gears. "I got an opportunity, man. Things are going to turn around for me. I just wanted to let Mr. Benelli know."

"I'll tell him."

Tex glanced at me. "It's—it's a good thing, you know . . ."

"Sure, Tex," Largo said, after eyeing me for a second. "First of the month is coming up."

"Yeah, yeah, I know. I got it covered. I do."

"Okay, Tex." Largo shrugged his shoulders, shifting his coat on his broad frame. "That it?"

Tex shifted his weight back and forth, leaning to his left so he could look into the TV room. "Yeah . . . Yeah." He looked at me, as if I was supposed to jump in and save him. "Just let him know, okay?," he continued. "I got a thing I want to—"

Largo patted Tex lightly on the cheek with a large hand. "I'll let him know." He eyed me again and then went back into the TV room, where he sat back down on the couch. He didn't make any effort to talk to Track Suit.

I watched the back of Largo's head for a minute, sorting out some ideas as to what had just happened, and when I turned to ask Tex a leading question or two, he wasn't standing next to me. He had, in fact, disappeared. Where the hell had Tex gone?

The hall led to the main part of the house, where a bunch of people were standing around, pretending to listen to idle conversation while simultaneously striking poses and checking everyone else out. It was a typical Hollywood party, in other words. I scanned the sea of beautiful faces for my bug-eyed friend, wondering how he had managed to scamper off so quickly on me.

How much do you owe, Tex? was one of the questions I wanted to ask.

Tex's grand idea wasn't working out so well in my head.

I recognized a director and a couple of actors. The director was fatter and wrinklier; the actors were still tanned and toned, but their skin was stretched tighter. One of the women had gone up more than a few cup sizes. You'd need both hands now if you were going to—

"Butch? Butch Bliss? Is that you?"

A redhead with a sensual mouth and a plunging neckline on a skin-tight dress pushed her way through the crowded living room. Her physique was the reward of a rigorous gym schedule, and her legs looked great. Her heels gave her an extra six inches, and she could nearly look me in the eye. "It is you," she said when she had extricated herself from the crowd.

"Hello, Dahlia," I said. "You look good."

She put a hand on her hip and tossed her hair as she cocked her head. "Is that it? 'You look good, Dahlia.' Seriously?"

"I'm going for stoic understatement," I said. I didn't want to be rude—she looked amazing, truth be told—but the noise and the crowd were making me twitch, and I really wanted to find Tex. I really wanted to get out of this place. I didn't need to be here. This was a bad idea, letting Tex talk me into coming to this party. Especially with how that *meeting* had—

"Hey." Dahlia grabbed my shirt and pulled herself against my chest. "I'm happy to see you too, you big idiot." Before I could reply, she thrust her mouth against mine.

I kissed her back. As Tex kept insisting, I wasn't dead, and she felt good against me. Warm and soft and firm in all the right ways. She made a tiny noise in her throat as my hands went around her waist, and her hips pressed against mine. Wiggling as she felt me responding to her presence—it didn't take much; I was already half-primed from everything else I had seen. Her mouth parted and her tongue flicked against my lips, which were tingling from her contact and the buzzy taste of booze. My hand slipped down to cup her ass, and the hum in her throat increased to a delighted purr.

She broke contact first—a consummate professional, this one—and looked me in the eye as she licked the corner of her mouth. "You kiss like a recovering alcoholic," she whispered. "Trying so hard to be straight and true." She tapped her hip against me with *hard* and *straight*. I tried not to notice, but who was I kidding?

"Straight and true," I said, riffing on a line from the first movie we had done together. She played the roller skating carhop with the heart of gold. I played the down-on-his-luck semi-pro bowler, waiting for his chance to shine. Together, we got naked in the bowling alley.

She ran her hands lightly across my chest. "How long have you been out?"

"Since this afternoon," I said.

"You look good too." Her fingers traced the contours of my torso. "You didn't get soft."

"Neither did you." My hands were still on her waist and I squeezed her gently.

She made eye contact again. Her pupils were big and black, further evidence that she had been drinking a while. "You think anyone would notice if we did it right here?"

"I think everyone would notice."

She made a face. "Ugh. So many voyeurs."

"It's part of the business."

Her lips curled up again. "Not for me," she said. "Not anymore."

"Really?"

"I got out, Butch. Got myself a good agent. A couple of made-for-cable action movies. Three episodes in a network show last year. Option for more."

"Good for you, Dahlia."

She giggled. "I haven't had to take my top off for a year now."

I glanced down at the fabric of her dress, which was stretched tightly enough across her breasts there wasn't much left to the imagination. She looked down too and then pressed her breasts against my shirt. Her nipples rubbed against me. "You remember what they feel like, don't you?"

I needed to find Tex. I needed to get out of this place. I needed to go somewhere quiet. Somewhere with less people. Somewhere I could breathe.

"Dahlia . . ." I extricated myself from her embrace. "Have you seen Tex?"

"Tex? Tex Western?" Her eyebrows pulled together. "Dexter?"

"Yeah, Dexter."

She was reluctant to let go of my arm. "Such a little prick. If he's here, I'm sure he's crawling around on his hands and knees, sucking—"

I smiled pleasantly as I slid my arm out of her grip. I wrapped my hands around her fingers. "He's my ride," I said. "I need to make sure he doesn't leave me here."

"Oh, I'll give you a ride, Butch," Dahlia said. "I'll give you a much better ride . . ."

I couldn't help but recall what Tex had said about Dahlia when we had been sitting in the car at Tehachapi. *My one chance . . .* I squeezed her fingers. "Maybe later, Dahlia."

Her gaze sharpened, and something hard put a crease in her pretty mouth. "You were a good man, Butch. Too good for all of this."

I gave her an honest smile, letting her see a little of the confusion she was causing in my heart. "I was young and dumb," I said. "We all were. It's easy to mistake that for something else."

Before she could argue otherwise, I let go of her hand and darted off. Looking for Tex was my excuse, but seeing Dahlia was too much too soon. I couldn't take it anymore. I needed to get out of that place.

CHAPTER 5

I CUT THROUGH A KITCHEN THAT LOOKED LIKE IT HAD BEEN SWIPED from some cable cooking show, and wove through another long room with more bodies than places to sit, and finally emerged outside again. The pool was on my left, and it was round at one end and long and skinny at the other. There were two satellite hot tubs at the round end, and both were overflowing with naked people. I smiled and nodded as I strode past, my gaze still roaming around for Tex.

There were three cabanas past the pool, and the first one was filled with people having a good time. The other two were closed, but that didn't mean there weren't people inside, doing who knew what—though my imagination, no longer trapped in a six-by-nine cell, was starting to get some ideas. Past the pool, the trees closed in, and a couple of paved paths led off to more private spots on the property. I took a path—I couldn't tell if it was less or more traveled—and walked far enough into the trees that I could no longer see the party. I could still hear it, but at least I was only being bludgeoned across one sense instead of all of them.

A wooden bench was tucked next to a stone wall, and I sank down on it and put my hands between my knees. I was shaking, and my breath was coming too quickly. My flight response had kicked in, and I had let it take over, and part of me was jumping up and down about the fact that I could flee—that I could get away from all of the people—and the rest of me was scared shitless.

I wasn't afraid to admit it. I knew it was going to happen. You don't go from living in a tiny cage to wandering aimlessly around the big old world without some degree of transitional anxiety. Many ex-cons couldn't handle it. The freedom was too much. The myriad of choices—all of which you had to make now—were overwhelming. And, like Halter had said as I was checking out, these guys came back. They preferred a life inside to a life out, and, well, it didn't take much to get back in.

This isn't your life, Mr. Chow had said to me one afternoon when I had expressed some apprehension about my upcoming release. *You were a tiny larva when you came here. You have wrapped yourself in a cocoon and soon it will be time for you to be reborn. Like a butterfly.*

The prison shrink—a pinched-face man with a penchant for polyester and stripes—had said the same thing during one of the mandated psychological appointments required by the State of California before they let me leave. *You've educated yourself during your time here, Robert. You haven't frittered it away. You're ready to re-enter society. Be a productive member of your community.*

That isn't your life either, Chow had said.

What is my life? I asked.

What did you want to be when you grew up?

A movie star. That's why I came to Hollywood.

And were you?

I did a bunch of films I hoped my mother would never see, I said.

My trial made the *LA Times*. I'm sure the local paper back in Colorado picked it up. During the first year in prison, I had tried to write my mother a letter a few times. I never finished it. What was I going to tell her?

I taught you how to survive in here, Chow said. *It's up to you to figure out how to survive out there.*

Without you.

Every son leaves home. Every father knows this, from the day he becomes a father. It's part of who he is. Just as it is part of who the son is. Why did you leave Colorado? Not to spread your father's name. No. You left because it was time for you to make your own way in the world. This is no different.

This is different. I'll be an ex-con.

No, Chow said. *There is no ex. Are you an ex-son? There is no leaving behind what you were before. It remains part of who you are.*

So what am I supposed to do?

You are supposed to live, Robert.

Chow was doing ten to twenty for financial crimes: money laundering, wire fraud, tax evasion. The State of California sent him to Tehachapi instead of someplace more country club because of his Triad connections. Well, suspected Triad connections. They couldn't prove anything definitely in that regard, and so they settled for trying to break up the money. Chow ran a string of nail salons and convenience stores in LA—the sorts of places where there were lots of transient customers and variable income. The sorts of places that the DA's office like to think were busy washing money and banging out drugs bundles in the back room.

I had gotten five years for the drugs in the car, and no one cared about my opinion in that matter. The DA, however, did care about the horrific damage being done to the fabric of our society by the adult filmed entertainment industry, and yeah, Tex was right in that regard: my chances had been fucked from the get-go. My lawyer did what he could, but the DA was all starry-eyed about this ruinous intersection of drugs and porn getting to do some hard time. And I'm sure he got a secret thrill every time he said those two words.

Anyway, I was six months in when Lando came for me in the shower. Chow had come to my rescue, taking Lando's shiv from him, and puncturing the black man in four places before disappearing like a ghost. I had been left standing there, me and the dead guy, both naked, as blood circled the drain in soapy lines.

My nickel became a dime, and after a probation hearing that had turned into a circus, I decided to wait out my decade of State-mandated incarceration. There was no point going through the scathing ridicule of sucking up to a parole board who were prejudicially dismissive of the idea of personal rehabilitation.

There is no ex. Once a convict, always a convict.

Once a filthy pornographer, always a filthy pornographer.
Once a failure as a son, always a failure . . .

It's an endless litany, really. One I had learned like a mantra during my first month in prison. I would recite the lines out loud to myself after the lights went out. I would whisper them in the chow line, making the words seem more dangerous and deadly than they were. I scratched them into the brick wall next to my private shitter.

Once in prison, always in prison.

That's not very helpful, I told Chow when he said this.

I'm not in prison, he said. *My body may be here, but my mind and spirit are with my family. They can poison me with their food, strap me into my cot at night, and wipe my ass when I'm too old to sit on the toilet myself. But they can't hold me here.*

Where are you?

Chow had smiled and pointed up at the ceiling of the reading room. *Out,* he said. *I'm not in; I'm out.*

My chest ached, and my breathing was still too fast.

I was out, but I was still in.

Every morning, when we first got out to the yard after breakfast, Chow would lead us through our tai chi exercises. It was all about remembering how to move our bodies. How to breathe. How to feel a connection between our heads, hearts, and toes.

Prisons are built to break you. You get the mono-color jumpsuit. You get a number. You get a tiny room with grey walls and grey bars. You get fluorescent lighting, which slowly leaches all the life out of your skin. You get nothing, and even then, they threaten to take that away from you should you display the barest hint of will or identity or motherfucking rage.

Chow taught us how to connect with that thing they couldn't take away from us.

Over the years, we all led the morning routine. We were all students in our own bodies. We were all on equal footing in this vast cosmos. We were wind and stone and leaf. Individually and together.

The DJ was pumping out some off-kilter groove that kept bouncing back on itself—the sort of shit that makes the old folks complain about the noise kids these days listen to—and if you tried dancing to it, you'd probably snap a bone in your leg or something. It was the soundtrack to the broken, cut-up chaos banging around my head, and it got into my bones. I couldn't sit anymore, and so I stood up and worked on finding myself again. Moving slowly. Listening to my body and not the echoes hammering around by the beats. I carried water to the mountain. I lifted the tiger, and plucked plums like monkeys do. I soared like a crane and rolled like a leaf on the river. I became a cloud and let the sun blow me across the sky. And when the song rose to a banging climax and then shattered like a million picture windows coming down, I was left floating, a feather slowly gliding down from the apex of heaven.

I landed gently, and my hands were limp at my sides. The tension in my back was gone. The little lizard who wanted to flee had crawled back under the rock down at the base of my brain. My head was right once more.

It was time for me to go. I didn't owe Tex anything, and I certainly didn't need to *take a meeting* or whatever the hell that had been with Largo. I didn't know what he was doing, but it was obvious that he was in some shit. Clearly he was hoping that I was going to help him out, but I couldn't fathom how.

Well, there was one way I could help, and I wasn't interested. I would have told him as much if he had asked in the car, and it would have saved us both a bunch of trouble. But he had known that, which was why he hadn't asked. He had hoped all this—the noise, the booze, the pussy—would change my mind.

He had hoped that, out of prison, I would have been eager to get back in to the old business.

I'm not in; I'm out.

What are you going to do first? Bob had asked. Back in the yard.

I'm going to live, is what I should have said. *I'm going to make my own choice.*

I wandered back toward the party. I was going to do one pass through the house, and if I didn't see Tex, I was going to walk out the front door. Because I could. I could walk anywhere I wanted. The guys at the cab stand could call me a cab.

The sky was fading—purple and black—and shadows were starting to gnaw at the pretty colors glowing on the

49

rocks. The DJ wore a crown of white lights, and he looked like a ghost bobbing up and down in his booth. There were more people in the pool now, lots of pale legs kicking and squirming in the yellow- and blue-lit water.

I spotted Dahlia right before I spotted Tex. She was standing near the open doors of the house, backlit like on a movie lot. He was next to the bar on the other side of the pool from the cabanas, talking with a woman in a lime-green bikini. Shaking his hips and pointing at her. Still wearing his bug-eyed glasses. The woman in the bikini was tolerating his antics, and I paused near the cabanas to watch him for a second. I was also out of Dahlia's line of sight.

Our conversation hadn't ended the way she wanted, and that wasn't sitting well with her.

Two figures moved in straight lines, which made them stand out in the curious confusion of the party-goers. Largo and another hard guy. They had a specific destination in mind, and when Tex spotted them, he realized they were coming for him. Lime-Green Bikini was startled when he bolted, as were the two guys. They didn't run, but they picked up their pace. Tex went around the end of the pool, and darted to the left, taking one of the paths into the trees.

I drifted in that direction, but not in any hurry. I didn't want to draw attention to myself.

Largo elbowed past the girl in the bikini, and his pal shoved her hard enough that she stumbled into the pool with a squawk and a splash.

The noise drew some attention, but it wasn't the first time someone had fallen in the pool, and wouldn't be the last. No one cared all that much, especially when the girl bobbed up and started shouting at the guy who had shoved her.

I was on the other side of the pool. Not invisible. Just directly past the girl if you were standing on the back patio of the house, looking toward the excitement. Which was where Dahlia was standing.

We made eye contact.

Largo and his pal reached the end of the pool and ducked down the path Tex had taken.

"Shit," I said.

I hurried after them. I didn't look back at Dahlia.

The California Department of Corrections and Rehabilitation was oddly progressive in some areas—inmate education, for example. Tehachapi had a decent library, and there was an intra-library loan program that was a dangling carrot for the educationally-curious inmates. Once it was obvious I wasn't going to become a crack jailhouse lawyer, I started on a broader education. Got caught up on my classics, which is where I learned about Theseus, the Minotaur, and the labyrinth. The labyrinth was supposedly so complex that its maker—Daedalus, whose son had some problems with following directions—almost couldn't find his way out after finishing it. Yet, the way Theseus found his way down the heart of the labyrinth, where the Minotaur lived, was to not stray left or right. The labyrinth, while complicated, only has one path.

Mazes, on the other hand, are meant to confound you. Branching paths. Dead ends. Routes that loop back on themselves. In the fall, farmers cut complicated mazes through their corn fields and charge townies ten bucks a head to go get lost. Many of them do, and they wander around for hours out in the corn, before eventually finding their way out. *Best family day trip ever!* Dad says, over and over again during the drive home that night. The kids—sunburned and sugared to their eyeballs by Mom, as an apology for Dad's lunacy—sulk in the back, hoping to never leave the city again.

I felt like one of those kids as I stumbled along the paths behind the pool. Whose fucking idea was this outing? And why hadn't these jackasses been abandoned in their own damn maze? There was no coherence to the paths. I took two lefts and found myself staring at a tall hedge. I backed up, heard voices off to my right, and had to go a long ways to find a route that looped back that way. And when I heard the voices get more strident, I decided that the landscaper's design could go fuck itself and I shoved my way through the nearest hedge.

The trees muffled most of the music, but they also made it hard to figure out where the voices were coming from. I blundered through the brush, thrashing about like a moose, and I finally broke through onto another path. The voices had stopped, and I stood in the path for a moment, listening.

Thump thump thump went the bass.

A woman raised her voice off to my right. Just once.

I looked to my left. The path wound ahead and then turned past an old oak. I went down to the tree and turned. The path led to an overlook with a wooden railing. The ground dropped away past the railing, tumbling into a narrow ravine. There was a small stream down at the bottom of the ravine, and there was something blocking the flow directly below the spot where I stood.

Tex stared up at me. He wasn't wearing his glasses any more. One of his eyes looked at me. The other one looked somewhere else, and his eyelid was a puckered line of scar tissue. His mouth was open, but he wasn't breathing.

CHAPTER 6

"THERE YOU ARE."

Dahlia was delighted to have finally cornered me in a private location. Her mouth stretched into a wicked grin as she walked slowly toward me. Stalking me like I was prey.

"Dahlia—" I started, but she darted forward the last few steps and pressed me against the railing.

I panicked for a second, wondering if the wood was going to hold. It did, and I barely let out the breath I was holding before she crushed her mouth to mine. Her tongue was more insistent this time, as was the motion of her hips.

"There's no one watching us now," she whispered when she was done licking my teeth and tongue. "Let's do it right here."

"Actually . . ."

She stopped. "What?" There was fire in her eyes.

I nodded toward the ravine. "Though, watching is a relative term."

She peered over my shoulder and let out a tiny shriek when she saw Tex's lifeless body. "Oh my god!" She went rigid against me. "Is he . . . ?"

"I think so."

"Did you—"

I shook my head. "I found him right before you found me."

She buried her head against my shoulder, and I carefully moved us away from the railing. She let me guide her, and after a moment, I realized her resistance was more making contact with me than being paralyzed with shock. I gripped her shoulders and she lifted her head. Her eyes were big and dark, and her mouth was open suggestively. She started to smile as I looked at her, and her thighs wrapped around my leg. "Come on, Butch," she whispered.

"He's dead," I said flatly.

"And we're not. Isn't that the best reason? We're still alive. Why shouldn't we fuck?"

"He was my friend."

She grimaced. "No, he wasn't. He was going to use you like he did everyone else. Don't be naive."

"He gave me a ride," I said. "He picked me up."

"You let yourself get picked up," she said. "Like a farm boy, just off the bus."

I shook my head.

"Oh, Butch. He brought you here. Why? Did he promise you a job? Did he want you to meet some people? Or did he just want to show you off?" She ran her hands across my chest. "I don't blame him. You are worth showing off." One of her hands slid down and went under my shirt, and I shivered at her touch on my naked skin. "How long has it been?" she whispered, her lips close to mine. "How long has it been since someone touched you like this?"

"It's not why I'm here," I said thickly, moving my lips as little as possible. I could feel hers brushing mine as I spoke. Too much more of this and I would be done talking.

I tried to think of something other than the sexy woman pressed against me. Her hand had reached my nipple, and she tweaked it lightly, sending a *zing!* of electricity up my neck. She laughed at my reaction, her tongue flicking out and licking the corner of my mouth. Her other hand started snaking down, her fingers fumbling with my belt.

Tex, cockeyed, staring up at the sky. Tex, the feisty pain in the ass, who had launched his own series out of sheer tenacity. He wasn't pretty. He didn't like the gym. He wasn't even that well-endowed. He just liked being naked with women. And to make that happen, he sold himself to a studio. A couple of guys, running a shop out of an industrial warehouse in West Hollywood. Dongle Studios. Innuendo intended. Tex showed up with assless chaps, a g-string, and a cowboy hat. He told them how he had a loaded six-gun and he could fire it as long as they had film in the camera.

They shot *Cowpoke* the next afternoon. It was edited in a few days, and we all saw it a week later, dubbed onto a cheap videotape with audio that never quite synched up. It didn't matter, because we were watching Tex Western get naked with women.

Dongle made a lot of money with *Cowpoke*, and they rushed *Cowpoke 2* and *3* out as fast as they could. Tex had just finished shooting *Cowpoke 4* a day or two before the party up in Laurel Canyon. The night he hadn't gotten in the car with me. The night he had his chance with Dahlia . . .

"What happened?" I asked her.

"What?" She stopped nuzzling my neck.

"Ten years ago. When I went out for drugs. Tex didn't come with me. He said he had a chance with you. He wasn't going to miss it, and who could blame him. But earlier, you called him a—"

"A little prick." Her fingers stopped fumbling with my belt. "Why?"

She slipped her hand out of my shirt and took a step back. "That was a long time ago, Butch. It doesn't matter anymore."

"It matters to me. The Tex I knew—"

She let out a hard laugh. "The Tex you knew," she snorted. "Jesus Christ, Butch. It's been ten years. Film died. Video took over. AIDS killed a bunch of us. And where were you?"

"I was in jail," I said. "You know that."

"For something you didn't do."

"That's not how the judge saw it."

"That's bullshit, and you know it. I know it. Tex knew it. We all knew." Her face wasn't as pretty as it had been a minute ago. "You ran away. Prison was just a convenient excuse."

"What? What are you talking about?"

"*Stroker Lane* was going to be huge. You were going to be bigger than Bobby. He had the name and that cock

57

of his, but you —you had that extra something . . . That fucking *aw shucks!* grin of yours. Those abs. God, and the way you . . ." She sighed, letting the silence speak for itself.

"It was just another movie, Dahlia," I said. "How many were we doing that month? It was just like all the others. Same story. Same faces. Just a different location."

She looked at me oddly. "It wasn't," she said quietly. "It wasn't like that for me."

"What?"

A tear tracked down her cheek. "You were my first, Butch."

"No way. What? You had done movies before that."

"Soft-core. Girl-on-girl. *Stroker* was my first big break."

I tried to remember the bowling alley shoot. I had been doing films for a couple of years, and landing the lead in *Stroker Lane* had been an accident. Bobby Banger had been the rising star in those days. I was the guy who was always in the background. It had been like that since we had both broken in. In fact, the only reason I took "Butch" for my screen name had been because the studio had balked at two Bobbies. *Come on, kid, face it: Bobby Banger is a great name. We don't need a Bobby Bliss. Keep the last name, but come up with something else. Bernard, or hell, Beavis'll work.*

We had shot *Stroker Lane* in a couple of days—midweek—because we had been able to get a deal on the bowling alley. I had done four movies since that one. There had been delays with the studio. Some bullshit with the director. I hadn't cared. I had gotten paid. People had seen rough cuts. I was getting better offers. I wasn't looking back.

But it had been something special, hadn't it? The story wasn't anything new. Change the names; keep the plot. It worked for Shakespeare. Hell, it worked for everyone—hack or highbrow alike. Stroker was a going-nowhere bowler. Working at a shitty bowling alley in a no-name town. Literally. We never bothered to name the town. Dahlia was the prettiest girl at the carhop, and she roller-skated her way into Stroker's life. She showed him how to dream big again. How to grab ahold of something like he meant it and roll like he didn't give a fuck about anything other than slamming those pins.

But that last day of shooting. When Stroker and his girl finally do it out in the middle of one of the lanes. When she says to him: *Oh, Stroker, fuck me like you bowl.*

"Oh, shit, Dahlia, I'm sorry."

She wiped at her face. "Yeah, I am too. Ten years is a long fucking time to wait." She laughed, but it sounded like a hiccup. "And here we are: you, me, and Tex. None of us got what we wanted. How about that?" She put her hands on her cheeks and pressed her fingers over her mouth. She struggled for a moment with what to say, and then just dropped her hands. "That's it," she said, punctuating her words with another hiccuping laugh. "He's dead. You've spent a decade in jail, and I'm—" She shook her head, and didn't bother to finish.

I took a step toward her, but she stopped me with an upraised hand. "Goodbye, Butch," she said. "I don't—just don't."

She walked away, and I didn't stop her.

I didn't know what to say if I'd tried.

It was dark by the time I found my way out of the maze. The party was still going. No one had missed us. The girl in the lime-green bikini was still in the pool, though she had lost her top and all the shrieking she was doing was for show. The DJ had dropped the volume a notch or two, but otherwise, the beats were still banging away. The song was something almost familiar yet completely alien, like a John Denver tune turned into some kind of rave anthem. Something out of time.

Like me. I missed most of the '80s. We got *Miami Vice* reruns in prison, and some of the noisier and dumber movies were screened one in a great while when no one had stabbed anyone in the cafeteria. But mostly, the decade slipped by, and we didn't notice. We didn't care. We weren't part of that world anymore, and many of us didn't have any plans to go back either.

See you next week, Halter had said to me when I had left Tehachapi. A confidence booster, there. But there was a strong statistical showing that he was going to be right. Could I deal with being on the outside, or would I come running back to my concrete mother? Let her wrap me up in her iron bars and hold me tight.

They can break your body. They can break your spirit, Chow said. *But they can only take your mind if you let them.*

I wasn't the only one who had been incarcerated over these last ten years. Tex had only ever wanted respect from his peers. Dahlia had only wanted to be loved. And what about me? What had I wanted? What had I been denied all these years?

Dahlia was at the bar near the pool. She had finished one drink and was in the process of knocking back a second when I walked up. She looked at me over her shoulder, a smoldering look made more savage by the heat in her gaze. She didn't say anything. I was going to have to talk first.

"Whatever happened to Bobby Banger?" I asked.

She frowned, her mouth tightening. "What?"

"*Stroker Lane* came out after I went to jail," I said. "I never heard how it did. But you said I was going to be bigger than Bobby. *Stroker* was going to change everything. But I wasn't there for it. So what happened? What happened with Bobby?"

She tipped her glass back and let an ice cube slide into her mouth. She chewed it into smaller pieces. "I married him," she said. She put her glass down on the counter and signaled to the bartender. "And one for him, too," she said when she caught his attention.

"No," I said. "I'm good."

She turned and leaned against the bar. "Then I'll drink it." She swayed for a second, and then focused on me. "Pussy," she said.

I knew this game, and there were two ways to play it. I stepped up to her and looked deep in her dark eyes. I let her see how I would play this game. She paled slightly and then stood up straighter, bracing herself against the bar. We stayed like that until the bartender brought two glasses over and put them on the counter.

"And then what?" I asked.

"It was an ugly divorce," she said, turning and picking up one of the glasses. Her shoulder rubbed against my chest. "I took everything because he was an asshole. Because he was—" She shrugged, which made her body rub against mine. "And then he was gone. Left LA. Selling cars in Florida or some shit. No one cares."

"And Tex?"

The glass paused for a second near her mouth. "He was kind to me. For a while."

"You didn't marry him."

She snorted. "I had learned that lesson."

"But he wanted you, didn't he? He wanted more of you than you were willing to give him. And so he tried to be someone else. Someone that you would want."

She didn't say anything, but she didn't deny it either.

"He owes this guy money. Benelli. He's here. Watching the game with his boys."

Dahlia nodded.

"What's his connection to Prengle? He's got money. He's got connections. But he's not making movies."

"Money makes everything happen," Dahlia said. "And sometimes money can make you think things are still happening."

"Is Prengle having money troubles?"

She waved her glass toward the pool and the house. "Does this look like he's having money problems?"

I looked to be polite. "His daughter is having a birthday party in the guest house, while he's got a full-on banger going on out by the pool. He's got gangsters all over his TV room, and they are more interested in football than the naked girls cavorting all over the place. And you're here. And not for old time's sake either, I'll bet, which means your agent said you need to be seen. Maybe talk with a few folks. Kind of like Tex was hoping to do."

She finished her drink and reached for mine.

"That reoccurring character isn't coming back, is she?" I asked.

"That fucking show. Its numbers are taking a dive. The studio is going to move it to Sunday night—you know, where they bury the shit they are contractually obligated to air."

I sighed and watched her drink. "No one gets what they want," I said.

She shook her head. "No one does, Butch. That's life on the outside for you."

"No one gets what they want on the inside either."

She lifted her glass. "Well, here's to everyone being fucked." She drained the glass and made to catch the bartender's eye again. I put my hand over hers.

"That's enough, Dahlia," I said.

She made a face and shoved me with her shoulder. "Fuck you, Butch. I can do whatever I want. You don't own me. You don't own shit."

I squeezed her hand. "Dahlia," I said gently.

She looked at me, swaying more this time. I waited for her to find her center and focus on me.

I smiled at her and held her hand tightly.

What are you going to do first?

That question, from the yard. Still going around in my head.

"Tex is gone," I said. "And we have two choices about how we're going to deal with that."

"Two? What choices?"

"We can walk out of here and pretend we never saw him down there. We can pretend he's gone. Like Bobby. Off to sell cars in Florida."

"Fucker," she slurred.

"Or we do right by him."

"How?"

I squeezed her hand again, keeping pressure on until she focused on my eyes.

"He was kind to us," I said. "He wasn't family, but he was what we had, wasn't he?"

A tear started down her cheek. "Yes," she whispered.

"So, let's take care of him, shall we?"

"Yes," she whispered again.

CHAPTER 7

I picked a small room without a lot of furniture and waited for Dahlia to do her magic. The bathroom had a separate chamber for the toilet, a novelty which I couldn't fathom entirely, even after I opened and closed the door several times. There were two large sinks in a marble-topped counter, and four large mirrors reflected back the rest of the room. I didn't look at them after my initial survey of the room. I didn't want to look too much at the face I saw there. The guy in the mirror had changed in the last ten years. Maybe not on the outside, but on the inside, he was different.

There was no sign of that *aw shucks!* grin that Dahlia had been talking about.

It took Dahlia about ten minutes to talk Largo and his buddy into following her into the bathroom. I was glad it didn't take longer. She could hold her booze, but I didn't want to stress that limit.

I stood behind the door, the metal towel rack in my hands. It had come off pretty easily, and it was cheaper than it looked, but it would do.

Dahlia sashayed in, swinging her hips and giving the boys a look that would melt a camera lens. They crowded in after her, eyes locked on her hands as she started to peel her top down. Largo jerked slightly when the door shut firmly behind him, and he half turned, sensing something wasn't right.

I caught him across the bridge of the nose with the metal bar. He staggered back, putting up his hands and trying to get his brain wrapped around the pain instead of the pleasure it had been thinking about. I shoved him, and he fell into the bathtub, banging his head hard against the tile-covered wall.

His friend was slower, and he hadn't figured out what was going on. I grabbed him by the back of his jacket and bounced him off the wall next to Dahlia. He started to squirm, and he was big enough I didn't want the hassle, so I hauled him over to the counter and tripped him. A hand on the back of his head ensured that his face went splat against the marble top, where he left a vaguely Rorschach-ian blood stain.

Dahlia was frozen, her left breast half untucked out of her dress. Her eyes were wide. Lots of white panic.

"Hey," I said softly, snapping my fingers until she focused on my hand. "You should go."

She nodded distantly, and started to drift toward the door.

I caught her before she got there and fixed her dress.

She focused on my mouth, unwilling to look around at the two groaning men. "Are you . . . ?"

"You should go," I repeated. "Call your agent. Get a lawyer. Just in case."

"Just in case what?"

I shook my head. There wasn't anything more to say. I quietly pushed her out of the bathroom.

When she was gone, I shut and locked the door. "So, let's talk about Tex Western," I said to the two goons.

"Who?" said the guy at the sink.

I hit him in the face with the towel rack. He collapsed on the floor, sobbing and blubbering as blood ran down his face.

Largo glared at me. "Yeah," he said thickly. "I know Tex."

"Good. That'll make this easier."

"What do you want?"

"I want you to tell your boss that you killed him."

Largo shook his head. "He jumped."

I looked over at the guy on the floor. His legs were stretched out in front of him. I smacked him on the kneecap with the piece of metal. When he got done yelling, I pointed at Largo with the towel rack. "Every time he answers wrong, I'm going to hit you. If you want to give me better answers, then I'll hit him."

The guy on the floor looked up at me, confused. "But . . . but if I give you good answers, why are you hitting him?"

"Because he's an asshole," I said. "What do you care about why I'm doing it?"

I couldn't see both of Largo's hands, which made me uneasy, so I grabbed one of the towels off the floor. I threw it at him, and he tried to bat it out of the way. By the time he was done, I had spotted the gun he had been trying to pull out of his coat pocket. I pinned his hand to the bottom of the tub with the rod, and picked up the gun before he could stop me. He started to sit up, and I hit him with the rack to keep him from doing something even more stupid.

I dropped the gun in the toilet, flushed it, and closed the door to the tiny room. "Handy," I said.

Poking my head around the corner to check on the guy by the counter, I asked him if he had a gun too. He shook his head vigorously. "You sure?" I asked.

He put his hands up.

I tapped the metal rack against the edge of the bathtub. *Ping. Ping.* The rack was already crumpled and bent out of true. It all looks good, but it's just cheap crap. Appearances are everything. Just like Dahlia had said.

"Let's start over," I said.

Ping. Ping.

"Which of you is going to confess that you killed Tex?"

"Fuck you," Largo said.

"Really?"

"Yeah, fuck you. What are you going to do to us if we don't?"

"You're a bad motherfucker, aren't you, Largo?"

He glared at me.

I looked over at his pal. "He's a bad motherfucker, isn't he?"

The other guy hesitated. He wasn't sure what would happen if he answered the question, or which answer was the right one. "He's . . . he's a bad motherfucker," he said.

"That's a good answer," I told him, and I hit Largo with the rack.

I smiled at the guy on the floor as Largo howled. "You see how this is going to work?" I said.

He nodded quickly.

"Good. So, you're going to tell your boss that you pitched Tex over the rail, right?"

He made me wait for it, but he nodded eventually.

I looked down at Largo. "This only works in your favor if you have two bad motherfuckers on your team," I said.

He glared, daring me to hit him again, and I didn't move.

I was good at waiting. Better than he was.

He hadn't done time. He wasn't as hard as he thought he was.

And when he realized that I knew it, the bluster went out him like air leaking from a balloon.

The two guys at the valet stand perked up as I walked down the driveway. "You need your car?" one of them asked.

"Nah," I said. "I need a cab. One of you have a phone or something I could use?"

The dark-haired guy with the wispy goatee dug a small device out of his pocket. He flipped it open and handed it to me. It had a small black and white screen on the upper half of the clamshell and the lower half had a phone number pad. I looked around for the iron numbers that identified the street address of the house, and when I had found them, I looked down at the phone again. I dialed three numbers and hit the button that started the call.

"What's your name?" I asked the guy who had given me the phone.

"Ah, Tim."

"Thanks, Tim."

The phone clicked and the police emergency operator answered, asking me to state my emergency. "Hi," I said. I rattled off the street address of the house. "There's a dead guy in the ravine out back, and a couple of dudes locked in a bathroom who really want to talk about what happened. It sounds like an accident, but what with all the drugs involved, who knows what really happened?"

The operator started asking a lot of questions.

"Oh, my name?" I smiled at the valet. "My name is Tim."

I tossed his phone back to him. "Thanks," I said, and I walked past them. The police operator was still talking. Tim and his buddy stared at me.

I kept on walking.

I had gone about a half mile down the road when I heard a car behind me. I stepped over to the grass along the side of the road to make sure they had room to pass. It was a grey pickup, hauling a white trailer behind it. The truck slowed to a stop, and the passenger window came down.

"Fancy seeing you again," Geo said.

"Fancy," I said.

We heard sirens, and as we waited, a trio of black and whites went screaming past, lights and sirens going.

"Looks like something exciting is happening back there," Geo said after they were gone.

"I don't think we're missing anything."

"You want a ride?"

"Sure."

She unlocked the door and I climbed up into the cab of the pickup. She waited until I had my seatbelt on, and then she put the truck in gear and eased it down the road.

"You weren't going to come back," she said after we had rolled past a few houses.

"You were leaving," I pointed out. "So it's not like I'm the only one who blew it here."

"True," she acknowledged.

"You want to try again?" I asked.

"Sure." She smiled at me. "Your friend called you Bliss. That's your last name, right?"

"Yeah. If we're on a first-name basis, you can use 'Butch.'"

"Butch," she said. "Not 'Robert'?"

"My mom calls me Robert," I said. "But she hasn't called in a while."

"My mom called me Georgina. But that was a long time ago. It's just Geo now."

"Geo. Three letters. That's easy."

Her eyes were bright. "You like things being easy."

I thought about Mr. Chow, still in prison. I thought about Tex, staring up at the sky. I thought about the shape of Dahlia's mouth. I thought about Dicky Boy and Tattoo Bob and Lin, and the families you chose versus the family you were born with.

I looked over at Geo and smiled. "I think I like riding with you, and that's good enough."

"I like that too," she said.

THE BUTCH BLISS SERIES

Butch Bliss is an ex-porn star, ex-con who yearns for the simple life in sunny Los Angeles. Unfortunately, there is always someone who needs a favor or two . . .

HIDDEN PALMS

What starts as a simple job of finding a retired porn star turns into a weekend of trouble with crazed bikers, dope fiends, and a doctor with too many degrees on his hands . . .

SNAKE ROAD

Butch is in a cherry red Mercedes with four co-eds and a eight foot python, crossing the border to Mexico. What could possibly go wrong?

THE RIGHT KIND OF SINNER

Butch is buying beer one night when masked men hold up the convenience store. It looks like random chance until Butch realizes one of the gunmen is an old prison nemesis with a score to settle . . .

Turn the page for a sample from HIDDEN PALMS, the first Butch Bliss novel.

CHAPTER 1

"What do you think of the view?" Matesson asked.

I was supposed to look at the waves rolling in, at the infinite distance to the horizon, and the fluffy white clouds towering up into the sky, but closer in, there was a blonde in the pool, wearing a tiny bikini. She was slumped on an inflatable dolphin; her head was back, and her eyes were covered by big sunglasses. Her hair trailed in the pool. The bikini top struggled to contain her, like trying to wrap your hand around an over-inflated balloon.

"Expansive," I offered. "You can see just about everything."

"Some days, when the wind comes in from the west, it's even more spectacular."

I glanced down at the inflatable dolphin again, and gave some thought to what would happen when the wind did come in.

"I appreciate you asking me to drop by," I said. "But it wasn't to see the view. Spectacular as it is."

Matthew Matesson let loose with a loud bray of laughter. In the pool, the blonde jerked slightly at the sudden noise, and there was a precarious moment where she might fall off the dolphin. She wiggled her hips a few times, finding a safe spot on the slick surface. I preferred watching her instead of Matesson anyway.

He had gotten fat in the last decade. His hair had thinned out too, and the greasy ponytail hanging down between his shoulders looked like something a cat might barf up. He wore a chain of gold links that hung farther down his chest than anyone needed to know, with a matching bracelet of the same around his right wrist. His swim trunks were a size too small and a season out of date, but that had always been Matesson's style. *Never be the first*, he had been fond of saying, *but always be the last.*

Word was he was out of the adult film business these days. Producing indie films now. I suspected porn had paid for part—if not all—of this view, and I wasn't quite sure how the blonde fit in with earnest stories of heartbreak and emotional growth, but then, I had always been hired help. No one paid for my opinion. Then, or now.

His laugh subsided into a loose chuckle that made his shoulders quiver. "Man," he said, looking down at the blonde, "those hips—"

"Why am I here?" I asked, interrupting his train of thought. I didn't need more details. My imagination worked fine. It didn't need any help from him.

"Why are any of us here?" he asked, and he laughed again at my expression. When I turned to go, he reached for my elbow. "Hang on, Bliss. Don't be such an uptight ass."

Before I could say anything, the large glass door behind us slid open, and a blonde woman came out. She was a twin to the woman in the pool, though she wore a red bikini instead of a blue one. She was carrying a tall glass of murky liquid in either hand. "Here you go, Matty," she said, offering him one of the glasses. It had a straw wide enough for a small-caliber bullet.

"Thanks, doll," he said. He nodded at me. "And thanks for bringing one out for Bliss, too."

Her smooth and pretty face scrunched up for a second as she looked at me. "Bliss, huh," she said, and she made it sound like both a question and an expression of exasperation.

"Yep," I said. Making it sound like both an answer and an apology.

Without breaking eye contact, she lifted the glass in her hand and wrapped her lips around the straw. She sucked, dimpling her cheeks, and the level of goop in the glass dropped a finger's width. She released her hold with a loud pop—a sound I hadn't heard in awhile, not in any context like this one, for sure—and offered me the glass. She flashed Matesson a less-than-friendly glare, and then spun on her heel and marched back into the house. We both watched her go. The glass was cold in my hand, and I considered holding it against my forehead to cool me off.

"It's got ginkgo and spirulina and other shit in it," Matesson said. He sucked heavily on his straw. "Supposed to make you live forever. I don't know about that, but I do know that you're going to have the best shit of your life in about three hours."

I eyed the glass, not quite sure if I needed such an experience.

"It also puts extra lead in your pencil, for when you've got some creative work to do. Know what I mean?"

I took a cautious sip from the straw. The stuff was cold and tasted better than it smelled, which wasn't saying much. I coughed when a familiar burn hit the back of my throat.

"That's your body telling you that you need to drink this stuff more often," Matesson said.

"Is that what's going on?" I said. I took a healthier sip, and it went down easier this time.

"I figured you'd be all into this New Age healthy greens shit," he said, waving a hand in my direction.

The backhanded compliment was the best you could hope for from Matesson. Of course, I was in better shape than he was—always had been, in fact. That's what the talent does. Though, it wasn't that high of a bar to cross.

Besides, LA was a town quick to judge. No one took you seriously unless you looked like you spent most of your day in the gym.

"I stay away from refined sugar," I said. "And I get regular exercise."

"That's all?"

"That's all."

"Not doing any . . . ?"

I let the question hang there for a minute. *Any what, Matty? Porn? Drugs? Both?*

"Doing porn in prison isn't the same thing as performing for some direct-to-video compilation," I said, figuring I'd pretend he wasn't talking about drugs.

"No?" He sucked at his drink. "Too bad. I bet there's a market for that stuff. We could get there first. Totally own the space."

"You didn't ask me to come up here to talk about doing a Prison Gangbang series."

"You always have to think about the opportunities, Bliss," he said. "You never know when you're going to hit gold. You always have to keep an open mind."

I looked down at the blonde in the pool, and tried to leave my mind open, which was pretty easy when I was looking at her. "I'm going to finish this drink, and then I'm going to go," I said. I lifted the straw out of the glass, and held it over the edge of the balcony. Green goop dropped from the end and spattered on the white stone running around the edge of the pool. I let go of the straw, and watched it bounce on the stone.

I put my back to the balcony, and chugged half of the remaining contents of my glass. My throat burned, and my eyes watered, but I swallowed all the ginkgo and other shit. "You'd better start talking," I said, showing Matesson how much was left.

Matesson held up a hand. "Okay, okay. Jesus, Bliss. Don't be such a hardass."

I thought about the possible responses to that statement, and figured I should just keep my mouth shut instead. I gulped another mouthful of the green drink, and waited for him to say something interesting.

"Okay, okay," he said again. "Look. I have a little problem. It requires a bit of delicate handling. Know what I mean?"

I shook my head.

He blew out his cheeks, and looked out over the pool. Like he was actually staring at the ocean and not the stacked blonde in the pool. "Word is you're a guy who can help a guy. You know. A little side work. For cash. No questions asked. That sort of thing."

"You want me to kill someone for you?"

"Fuck! No. Jesus Christ, Bliss. Nothing like that."

"Good," I said. "Because that's really expensive."

He blinked at me, and actually got a little pale. He sucked on his drink for a minute. "Seriously . . . ?" he started, and then stopped. As if he was embarrassed to have been caught asking.

"Let's not go there," I said. Even though there was no there to go.

"Yeah, yeah, okay." He nodded vigorously. "Yeah, that's not what I . . . I just—Jesus, man, really?"

I gulped a quarter of the remaining drink in my glass. "Prison changes a man," I said, keeping a deadpan expression on my face. "Makes him think about what's really important. Life. Death. All that shit. Makes him wonder what he's capable of."

"Goddamn," Matesson whispered.

Jerking his chain would have been more entertaining if he hadn't been one of the assholes who had pushed me to make one of the dumber decisions during my young, dumb, and full of—well, *those* days. I didn't blame him directly. That would be failing to take responsibility for my own actions, and it's important for a self-made man to acknowledge the choices that make him who he is. But still, Matesson had been part of a chorus that had convinced a young and gullible mind to do some stupid shit. Messing with him now—thirteen years on—wasn't payback. That would be petty, and who has time for that shit?

Which made me ask myself why I had even bothered coming up to his house. I had put all that behind me already—shortly after I got out.

I finished the drink and put the glass on the edge of the balcony. "Thanks for the cleansing tonic," I said. "I'll be sure to thank you again in a couple of hours."

"Hang on, Bliss." He started to reach for my arm, and then caught himself. "It's not like that. It's not. Really."

"What isn't?"

"Look, I have a problem. I need someone who can take care of these sorts of things. Discreetly, you know?"

"I'm not sure I do."

"I need you to find someone for me."

"Who?"

"A friend."

"What sort of friend?" I nodded toward the pool. "Like her?"

"Nah." He inclined his head. "You remember Gloria Gusto?"

It took me a minute to put a face to the name. "Yeah," I said. "I do."

Gloryhole Gloria. Nicknames were a double-edged sword. They made you recognizable in a field that was constantly crowded with new faces, but they also became the only way you could be remembered. Some managed to rise above the names they got saddled with. Some owned them for all they were worth, knowing such celebrity was fleeting. Bobby had been like that. Once he had claimed his name, he had lived like a king for as long as he'd been able.

I hadn't been one of the smart ones, and it took a couple of years of incarceration before that really sank in.

Two things prison offered in abundance: time to think, and time to read. I had taken advantage of both.

"She could act, and she had a healthy set of lungs. Not surprising, really. Given the rack she had." Matesson nodded at some memory, a smile greasing his lips.

"She came with me," he continued. "When I got that deal with Showtime. It was late-night stuff. Low budget. Rubber suits. Knockoff effects burned in during post. But viewers knew she was going to lose her shirt. And man, not only could she scream like a banshee, but she had this way of wiggling her tits when she let loose. Suits loved it. Had me shooting a picture a month for them. We could have ridden that gravy train for years. But . . ."

He shook his head.

I remembered Gloria. The studio had rented this big house up in the Canyon for a month, and had been shooting there nonstop to save money. There were always at least two crews working in the house. I couldn't recall the name of the film I had been working on that day. Nor the plot. Not that either of those mattered. Who knew what the film would be called by the time it hit the shelves? Anyway, the AD from the other film begged me to come fill a hole. They needed a fifth. I had been tired. Strung out. And I hadn't been at my best.

But Gloria? She was kind and patient and a tireless performer. She made me look a lot better than I deserved that day.

"But what?" I asked Matesson.

"Breast cancer," he said. He grimaced, and sucked heavily at his drink. "They caught it early, but it wasn't the same after that. Not because"—he gestured at his chest—"nothing like that. She just didn't . . . Anyway, the gravy train ran out of gravy. Cable took off, and they wanted smut without anyone taking their clothes off. They wanted viewers to think about people fucking, but they wouldn't hire any of us because we had reputations for actually showing people fucking, and that wasn't what they could show on cable. Dirk got a series—shot a pilot and a few episodes—and then the suits got feedback from focus groups, and word was that the viewers felt ripped off. Those who knew Dirk from Pearlescent were expecting tits and asses, and all they got was push-up bras and lacy panties."

"Uh-huh," I said. The drink was starting to make itself felt in the base of my skull, and not for either of the reasons that Matesson had mentioned earlier. I wondered about the ratio of the ingredients in my glass. My mouth tingled, and I considered leaving Matesson on the balcony—he would probably continue his bitch session just fine without me—and asking the other blonde if she could make me another one of those drinks. *I have got to know your recipe. What's the ratio of rum to spirulina?*

"Anyway, Gloria's been kidnapped," Matesson said, snapping my attention back to him.

"Kidnapped," I said, somewhat thickly.

"Well, not exactly," he said.

"How inexact are we talking about here?" I asked.

"It's this place. Up north," he said. "Some kind of retreat center."

"An asylum?"

He shook his head. "Not like that. It's some sort of spiritual retreat. But the guy running it is some kind of guru. He encourages his devotees to remain close during their studies."

"But they can leave any time they want to, right?"

"Sure, but they don't want to."

"Ah," I said. "How long?"

"Eight, nine months now, I think."

"And staying at this retreat isn't free, is it?"

Matesson wandered up to the edge of the balcony. He looked down, drumming his fingers on the rail. "I'm not sure it's the best thing for her," he said. "These sorts of crackpots prey on the desperate and lonely. They offer hope. A promise of a better life than what you've got. Freedom from pain and hurt and all that shit. You know what I mean?"

"Sounds like something I heard once upon a time," I said.

His fingers stopped moving. "We were all young and gullible once upon a time," he said.

"And look at us now," I said.

He turned his head and squinted at me. "Go check on her for me, would you?" he asked. "She's at some place called the Hidden Palms Spiritual Center. Up north, somewhere in the San Rafael Mountains. Not far from some speck of a town called Sisquoc. Off the 101, near Santa Maria. Go, and make sure she's okay."

"And if she's not okay?"

His face tightened. "Bring her home."

"Home?"

"Back to LA," he said. "Where she belongs. Not up there, in the woods. With that quack."

"This guy's a duck?"

"You know what I mean."

I digested his request for a moment. "You going to cover my expenses?" I asked.

"Of course."

"What about incidentals?"

"You going to type up an invoice?"

"No."

"Then I'll take your word for it," he said.

I considered that. "I'll need some to start."

His face continued to screw in on itself, making him ugly, and then something inside him unwound, and his features relaxed. "Barbara will get you what you need," he said, nodding toward the house. "Just take care of this for me, would you?" He hesitated, waiting to see if I would say anything, and when I didn't, he pressed on. "You owe me, remember?"

I nodded. I had been wondering if that was going to come up, and now that it had, well, I guess I was going to take the job.

"I'll go talk with her," I said. I nodded toward the pool and the sea and the sky. "Thanks for letting me take a peek at the view," I said.

He tried for a smile, but failed to get it arranged properly on his face.

I left him there, brooding on the balcony above the pool with the blonde and the inflatable dolphin. I was struck by the idea that he hadn't liked recalling the debt between us any more than I had, which made me wonder what I was going to find up north. In the woods. With the quack.

Barbara was in the kitchen, watching a cooking show on a small television. I put the empty glass on the counter, and she looked up from the tiny screen.

"Not quite enough rum," I said.

She smiled at me, the tip of her tongue caught in the corner of her mouth. "There might be some left in the bottle," she said.

"Matesson said you were going to give me some cash," I said.

"And . . . ?"

"I suppose we could check the bottle after that."

Her smile widened, and she crooked a finger at me to follow her.

About the Author

Harry Bryant is the pseudonym of an author living in the Pacific Northwest. He is hard at work on the next book in the Butch Bliss series.

You can find out more about Harry's projects at his website.

http://www.harrybryantwriter.com